Christmas 20

TO: Noah, Max and Adam

A Gift From:

Uncle Chuck

Aunt "Cathy"

For Gene & Mary,
and Kristie

-SB

www.mascotbooks.com

The Adventures of Molly & Ollie: Moving Day

For more information, please contact:
Mascot Books
620 Herndon Parkway, Suite 320
Herndon, VA 20170
info@mascotbooks.com

Library of Congress Control Number: 2020914260

CPSIA Code: PRT1120A
ISBN-13: 978-1-64543-249-4

Printed in the United States

The Adventures of Molly & Ollie

Moving Day

Sally Beale

Sally Beale

Illustrated by
Cheryl Crouthamel

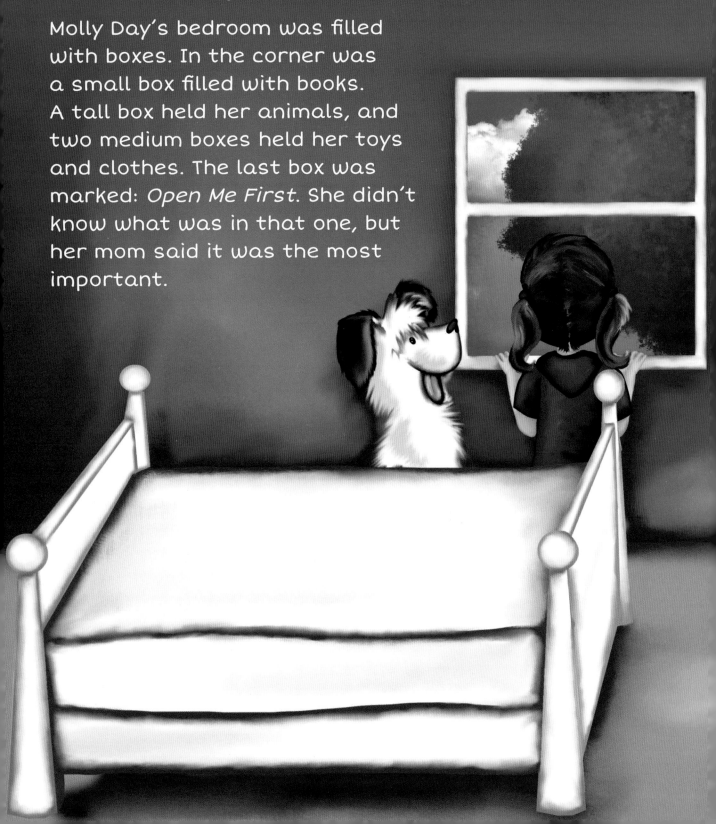

"Today is moving day," Molly sighed. "There's my backyard. I'll *never* play there again. And there's Becky's house. I'll *never* see her again."

Molly Day's bedroom was filled with boxes. In the corner was a small box filled with books. A tall box held her animals, and two medium boxes held her toys and clothes. The last box was marked: *Open Me First*. She didn't know what was in that one, but her mom said it was the most important.

"I don't want to move!" Molly moaned to Henri, her big black and white sheepdog.

Suddenly, the doorbell rang. **DING DONG!**

Molly raced down the stairs followed by Henri. Mrs. Day opened the front door and *giants* rushed inside!

Molly watched the whirlwind—trying to be brave—as several giants carried all the boxes and furniture out of the house and into a *huge* truck.

DING DONG! The doorbell rang again. "What did they forget?" Molly asked, looking around. "Everything is gone!"

"Becky!" Molly cried out, excited to see her best friend.

"I brought you some chocolate chip cookies," Becky said. "I know they're your favorite."

"Thanks, Becky!" Molly said as she stepped outside. Henri gave an excited **"WOOF! WOOF!"** in approval.

As they shared the cookies, Mrs. Day came out with her arms full of cleaning supplies. Molly's little brother, Jeffrey, was close behind. "Okay girls, time to go," she told them.

Molly looked around and sighed. "Everything is gone."

Molly watched out the back window of the car as Becky waved goodbye and her old house disappeared in the distance. Henri snuggled up next to her. "Nothing will be the same," she whimpered softly to him.

After a long ride, they parked in front of a big white house with a front porch. Molly dragged her feet as slow as a snail as she approached her new home. "I'm not in any hurry," she whispered to Henri.

There, Molly discovered a jungle of boxes! Everywhere!

"How do we walk around?" Molly cried.

"There's a path," said Mr. Day, showing her how to get through the mess. "Go upstairs and check out your new bedroom!"

Molly and Henri moved along the path and up the stairs. At the top of the stairs, she saw a door marked "MOLLY" in big purple letters. "There it is," Molly said.

"WOOF," Henri agreed.

Inside, she found the small box of her books, the tall box with her animals, the two medium boxes with her toys and clothes, and the box marked *Open Me First*.

Molly sat on her unmade bed and sighed. "Everything is different."

Suddenly, Molly heard a voice say, **"WHO?"**

Molly looked toward the voice and saw a little brown owl perched on her windowsill. **"WHO?"** the owl asked a third time.

"Who?" Molly asked the owl back, as she tilted her head to the side.

"Who are you?" the owl asked.

"Oh, I'm Molly, and this is Henri. Who are you?"

"I am Oliver Winston Howell III." As he said his name, the owl waved his wing in a large circle, and with a **ZIP! FAP! POOF!** his feathers changed to a shimmering brown. He was wearing a green plaid vest with a gold pocket watch and a polka dot bowtie.

"Nice to meet you, Oliver Winston Howell III," Molly said. "You know, that's a very long name. May I call you Ollie?"

Oliver Winston Howell III paced back and forth with his wings tucked behind his back. His feet went *click-clack, click-clack* as he thought it over.

"Okay, Ollie it is. And it's very nice to meet you, too," he replied with a deep bow.

"Where did you come from, Ollie?" Molly asked.

"See that large tree in your backyard?" Ollie said, waving his wing. All the leaves on the tree began to sparkle and shimmer in the breeze. "That's my home."

Molly's eyes grew wide.

Ollie hopped off the ledge and into Molly's room. "Why did you look so sad when I arrived?"

"Today is moving day!" Molly wailed. "Everything is different. I had to leave my best friend, my backyard, my bedroom. *Everything* is different!"

"Oh, my. Oh, my," Ollie said as he paced back and forth with his wings tucked behind his back. His feet went *click-clack, click-clack* as he thought it over.

KABOOM! Ollie bumped into a box with a loud thump. He looked around Molly's messy room. "Oh, my. Oh, my. What's in all these boxes?"

Molly pointed to the tall box. "Well, that's my animals and—"

"Animals? I must meet them!" Ollie said as he hopped up and down. He waved his wings, and the box popped open.

"**HOORAY!**" cheered the animals. One by one, a parade of animals came out of the box.

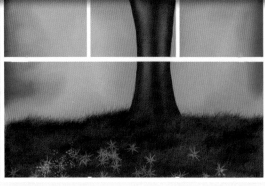

"Hi, I am Mia Monkey!"

"I'm Harry Hippo. I was a Christmas present."

"Roscoe Raccoon, at your service."

"*Oink. Oink.* I'm Penny Pig. I clean up real nice."

"I am Patty Panda. Glad to meet you."

"I...am...Timmy... Turtle. I'm a little slow, but you can count on me."

"I'm so pleased to meet you all," Ollie told them. He started pacing back and forth. His feet went *click-clack, click-clack* as he thought it over.

Henri barked, **"WOOF!"**

"Yes, of course. You still have Henri, too," Ollie said with a laugh.

Suddenly, they heard footsteps. "Oh, no! My mom is coming!" Molly exclaimed.

Mrs. Day opened the door and, quick as a wink, all was still. Ollie had tucked himself behind Roscoe.

"Molly, it's time to get ready for bed," Mrs. Day said, looking around the room suspiciously. "The *Open Me First* box has your bedding and pajamas."

"Okay, Mom," Molly replied, giving her an innocent smile.

Mrs. Day took one last look around and then closed the door as she left.

Then, quick as a wink, they all sprang to life again!

Ollie waved his wings and the *Open Me First* box popped open.

Henri barked, **"WOOF! WOOF!"** as the sheets whirled out of the box and around the room. The animals chased the sheets and made the bed, while Timmy Turtle slowly dragged out her pillow.

As the box emptied, Ollie saw something at the bottom. "What's this?" he asked Molly.

They all gathered around and peered inside the box. There was a new blanket with purple flowers that Molly had never seen before. A note was attached:

For Molly, Love Grandma

Ollie started pacing back and forth with his wings tucked behind his back. His feet went *click-clack, click-clack* as he thought it over. He said, "You know, Molly, your family still loves you, too!"

"Yes!" Molly agreed, as she took out the blanket and gave it a big hug.

After Molly put on her pajamas and brushed her teeth, she looked around at her new bedroom. All her clothes had gone into her dresser and closet. All her toys and books had found their place in the bookcase. And all the animals had settled in for the night.

"You're right, Ollie, not *everything* has changed," Molly said as she picked him up and gave him a little hug. "You know, Ollie, we're going to be best friends!"

She set him on the windowsill and then snuggled into her old bed with her new blanket. Henri curled up beside her. "Maybe it will be okay here after all," Molly said. "Goodnight, Ollie. See you tomorrow!"

"Sweet dreams, Molly," Ollie said. "Tomorrow is a new day and a new adventure!" Then Ollie flew back to his home in the shimmering oak tree.

Photo by Adrienne Reich Photography

About the Author

Sally Beale is a children's book author living in Raleigh, North Carolina. Before settling there in her early twenties, she had already lived in eight other states, moving every two years with her family. Her childhood was filled with adventures that captured her imagination in each new home. Sally continued her passion for adventure while raising her two daughters and working as a costume designer for local theaters. Now she is channeling her sense of fun and her youthful spirit into her children's stories. *The Adventures of Molly & Ollie: Moving Day* is the first book in the Molly & Ollie series.